D0928983
It's a book and card!
THE WAY TO OUTER SPACE
The card said:
Dear Em,
Please follow the instructions in
this book and come to outer space.

Who sent this?
THE WAY TO OUTER SPACE

It's silly!

But then, Em saw instructions to make a rocket.
Hmm. Maybe we should try it ...

MAKE a ROCKET

You will need:

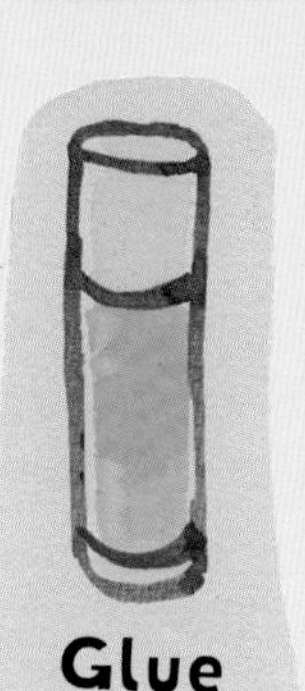

Glue

Sticky tape

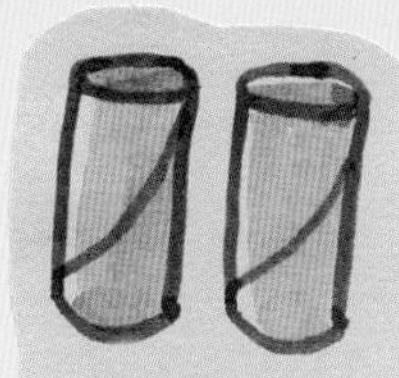

Two toilet rolls

Double-sided tape

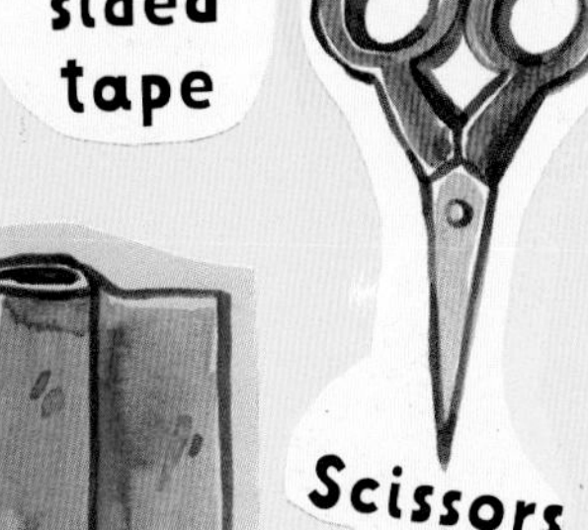

Scissors

Tin foil

Paper

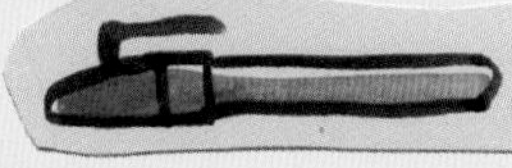

Marker

Colouring pencils

1 Collect two toilet rolls and stick them together with tape.

2 Spread glue over the toilet rolls and cover them with foil.

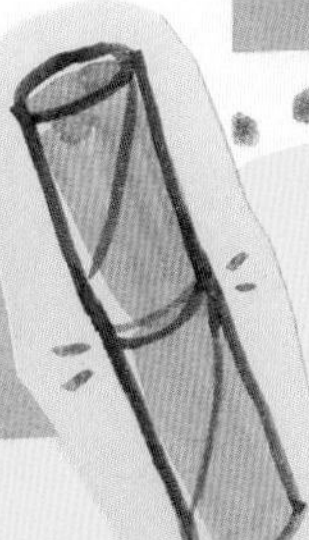

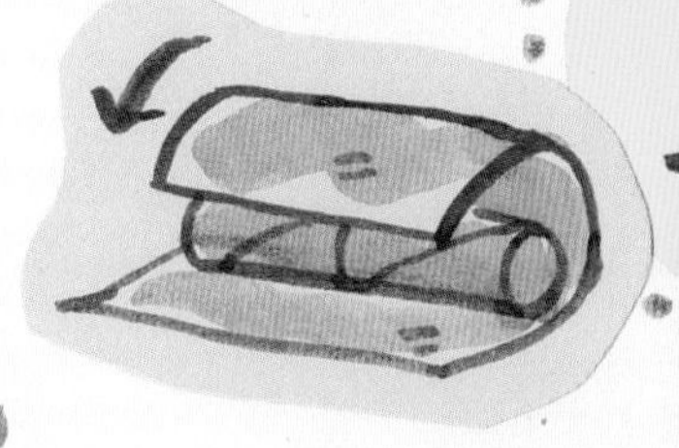

3 Find the templates on the next page and trace them onto paper.

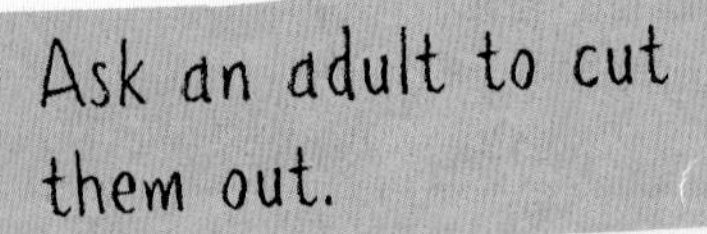

Ask an adult to cut them out.

4 Now colour them in! Roll the cone into shape and secure with tape.

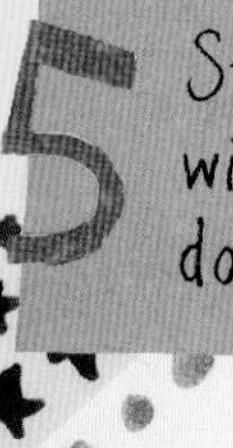

5 Stick the nose cone and wings to the rocket with double-sided tape.

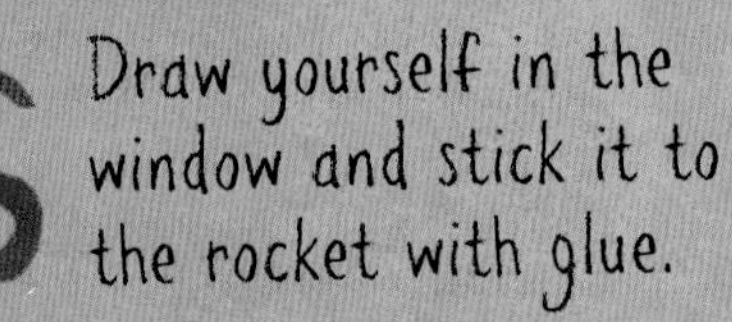

6 Draw yourself in the window and stick it to the rocket with glue.

ROCKET TEMPLATES

Trace the nose cone, wings, and window onto paper and cut them out. Then colour them in and follow the instructions to create a rocket!

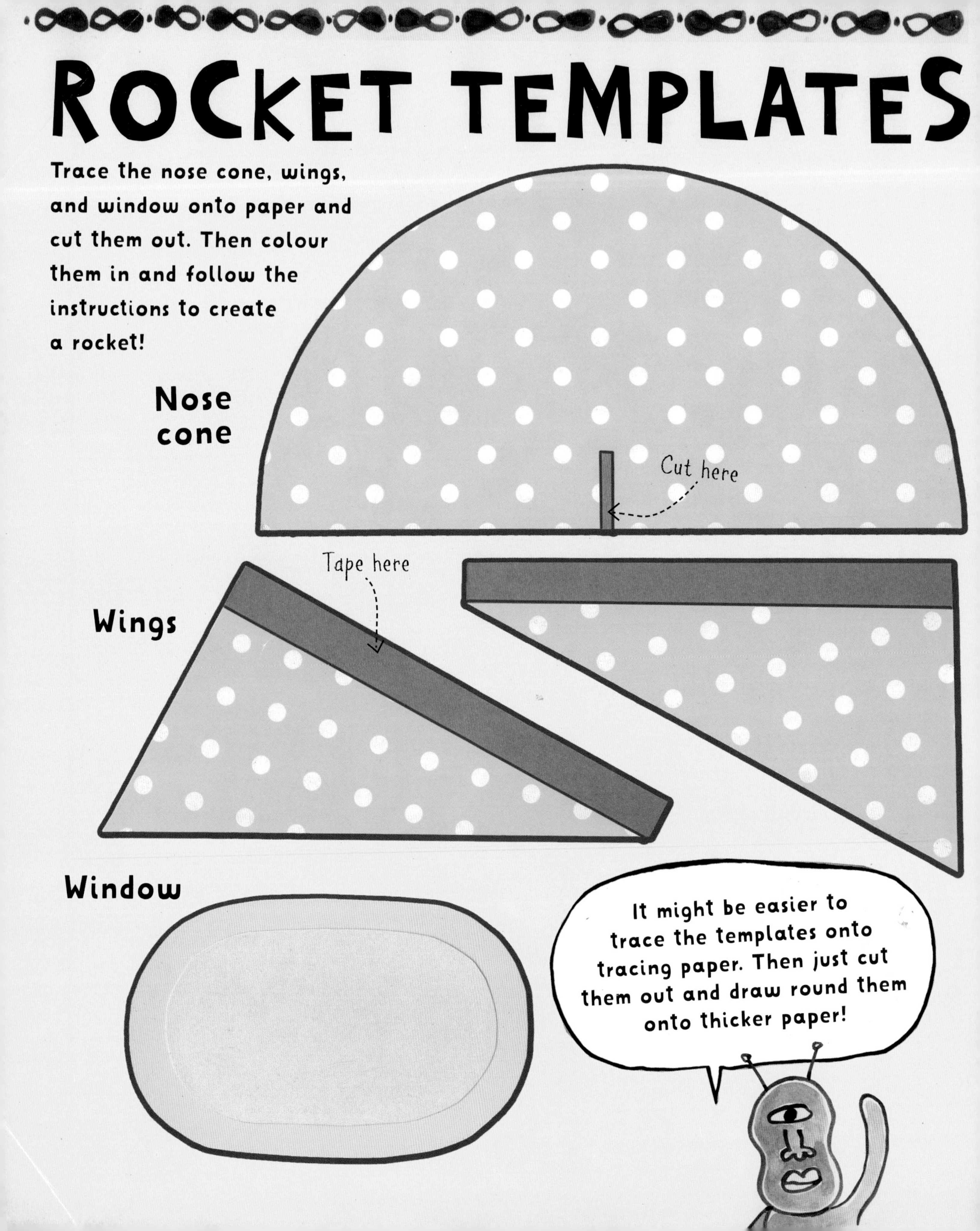

And soon ...
Yeah!
Done!
THE WAY TO OUTER SPACE

POP!

WOW.

Am I really in my rocket?

What's this ...?

It's taking off!

BLAST OFF!!
ZOOM!

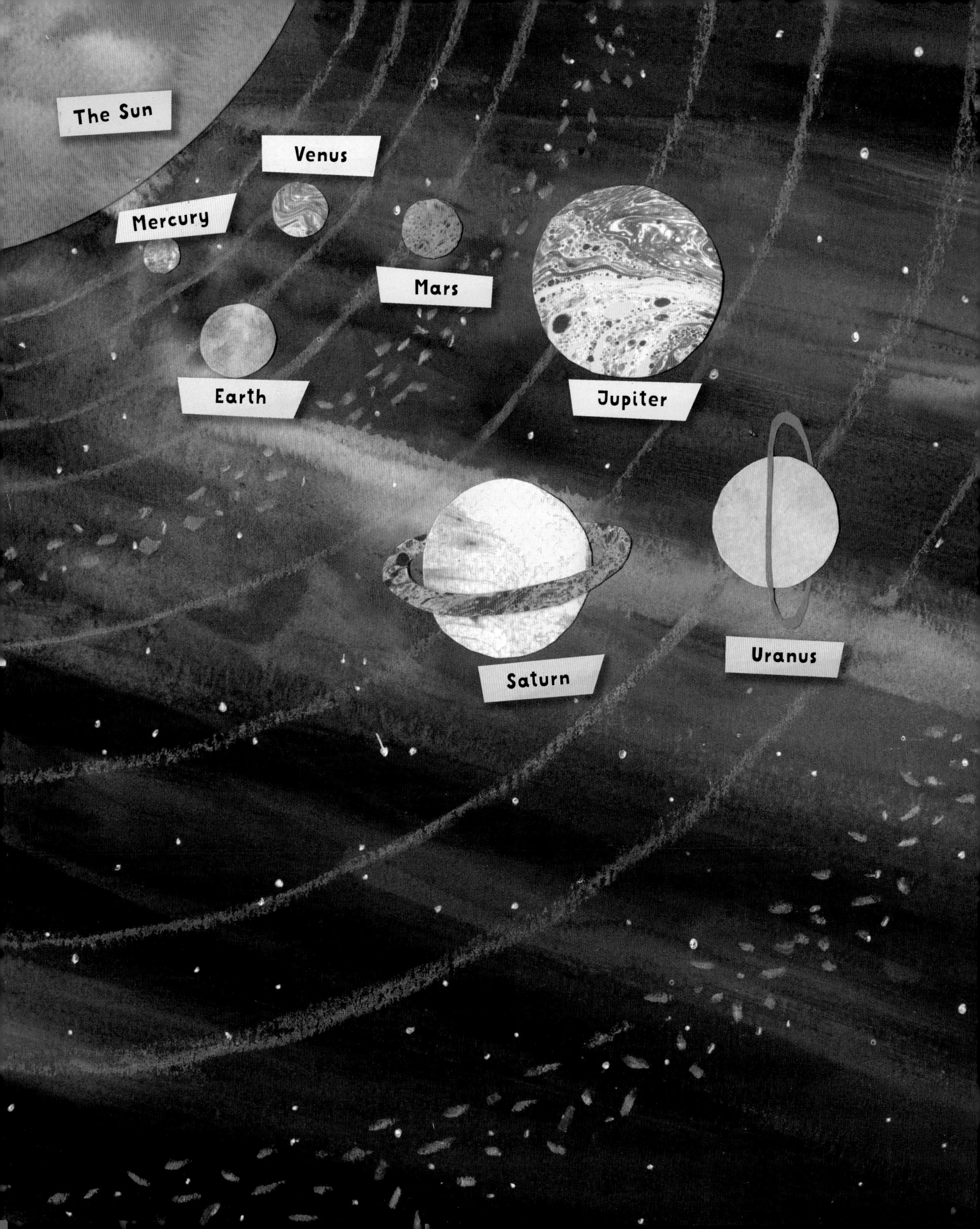
The Sun
Venus
Mercury
Mars
Earth
Jupiter
Saturn
Uranus

Pluto
Em's rocket hurtled through the whole solar system and out the other side. But where was it going?
Neptune
She's coming!

Wow!
But why is everything so GREY?

EM
What's that? EM? That's my name.

Hey, Em.

Welcome to YOUR planet!

My planet? Why is it mine?
Because we were made from YOUR imagination.
Do you remember when you created us?
You dreamed a whole world for us.

But recently you've been bored, doing nothing.
And never thinking about us ...
That's when our planet started to die.
Many of us have already left.
It's so mundane now.
I can't live here anymore!

That's why we sent our book to you.

Please can you use your imagination and save this planet?

There are only four of us left now.
We miss our alien friends. Can't you make us some more?

OKAY! I'll do it!

CREATE ALIEN FRIENDS

You will need :

Colouring pencils or pens // Paper

Here's an example

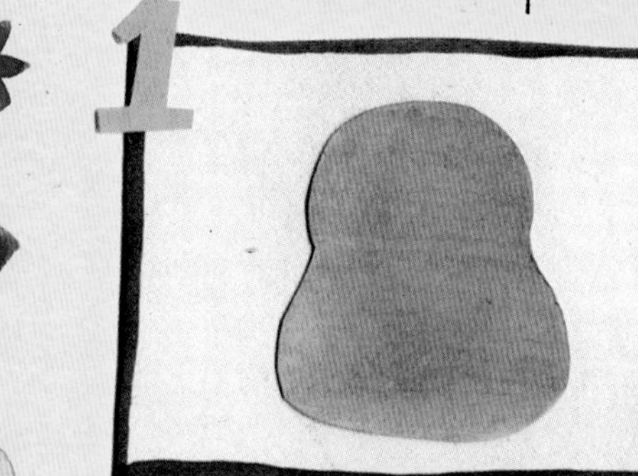

1. Draw a body for your alien friend.

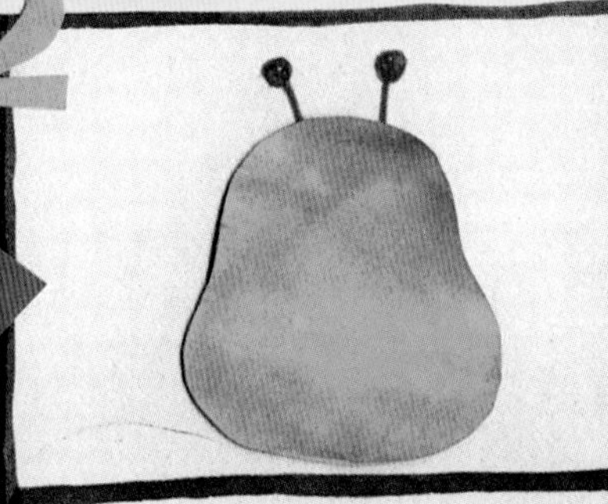

2. Add two feelers on the top of the alien's head.

3. Give the alien an eye or even two!

4. Draw the alien a nose and lips.

5. Add arms and legs. This alien has three legs!

6. Now you've made your first alien friend.

You can make lots of different aliens again and again. Let them come back to their planet!
WELCOME BACK!

Ta-dah!
Here are more aliens for you!
It's just like old times!

But!

It's still too grey!

What can I do to make it brighter?

Hmm.

Oh!

This planet needs more STARS!

ORIGAMI STARS

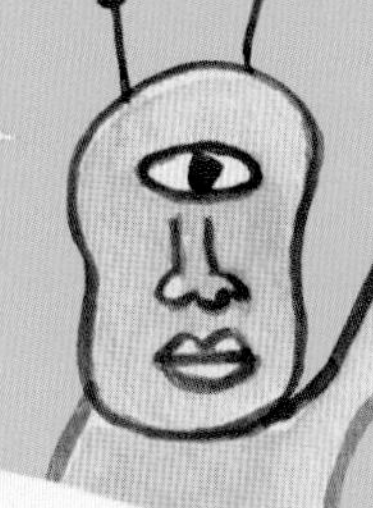

1

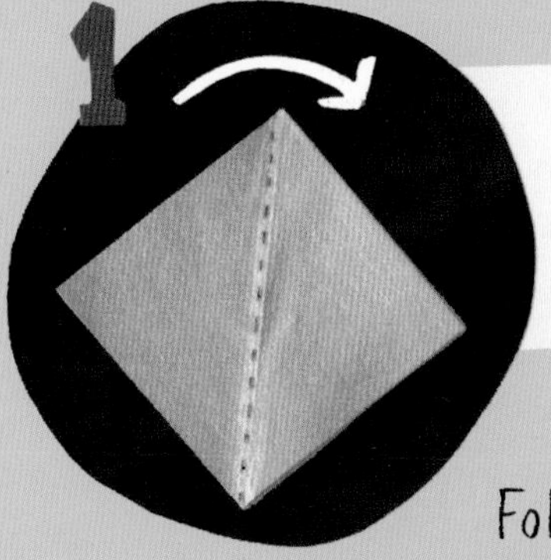

Fold a square of paper in half diagonally.

2

Then fold two more squares the same way.

3

Glue two of the pieces together, as shown.

4

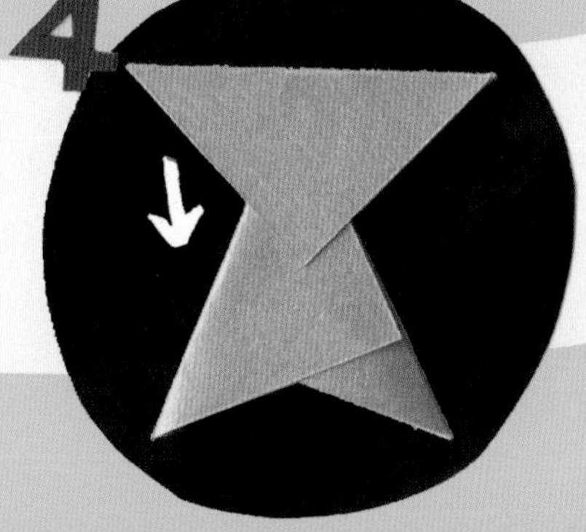

Then glue on the third piece like this.

5

TA-DAH!

You've made a star. Now make some more!

Now you are ready to make the alien planet brighter.

Make as many stars as you can!

Turn over the page and see the beautiful stars Em has made!

Wow, it's beautiful now!

Thank you, Em.

Don't forget to keep using your imagination.

Bye-bye.
Bye, Em!

ZOOM!

The next day, almost everything seemed the same ...

But things were very different in Em's bedroom ...

I'm going to make something AWESOME!
Where will Em's imagination take her next?

For my grandmother.

OXFORD
UNIVERSITY PRESS

Great Clarendon Street, Oxford OX2 6DP
Oxford University Press is a department of the University of Oxford.
It furthers the University's objective of excellence in research, scholarship,
and education by publishing worldwide. Oxford is a registered trade mark
of Oxford University Press in the UK and in certain other countries

First published in 2016

British Library Cataloguing in Publication Data

Data available

ISBN: 978-0-19-274476-0

1 3 5 7 9 10 8 6 4 2

Printed in China

Paper used in the production of this book is a natural,
recyclable product made from wood grown in sustainable forests.
The manufacturing process conforms to the environmental
regulations of the country of origin.